Dear Parents:

Congratulations! Your child is taking the first steps on an exciting journey. The destination? Independent reading!

STEP INTO READING® will help your child get there. The program offers five steps to reading success. Each step includes fun stories and colorful art or photographs. In addition to original fiction and books with favorite characters, there are Step into Reading Non-Fiction Readers, Phonics Readers and Boxed Sets, Sticker Readers, and Comic Readers—a complete literacy program with something to interest every child.

Learning to Read, Step by Step!

Ready to Read **Preschool–Kindergarten**
• big type and easy words • rhyme and rhythm • picture clues
For children who know the alphabet and are eager to begin reading.

Reading with Help **Preschool–Grade 1**
• basic vocabulary • short sentences • simple stories
For children who recognize familiar words and sound out new words with help.

Reading on Your Own **Grades 1–3**
• engaging characters • easy-to-follow plots • popular topics
For children who are ready to read on their own.

Reading Paragraphs **Grades 2–3**
• challenging vocabulary • short paragraphs • exciting stories
For newly independent readers who read simple sentences with confidence.

Ready for Chapters **Grades 2–4**
• chapters • longer paragraphs • full-color art
For children who want to take the plunge into chapter books but still like colorful pictures.

STEP INTO READING® is designed to give every child a successful reading experience. The grade levels are only guides; children will progress through the steps at their own speed, developing confidence in their reading.

Remember, a lifetime love of reading starts with a single step!

Visit us on the Web!
StepIntoReading.com
randomhousekids.com

Educators and librarians, for a variety of teaching tools, visit us at RHTeachersLibrarians.com

ISBN 978-0-553-52290-7 (trade) — ISBN 978-0-553-52291-4 (lib. bdg.)
Printed in the United States of America
10 9 8 7 6 5 4 3 2 1

nickelodeon

RUBBLE TO THE RESCUE!

by Kristen Depken
illustrated by MJ Illustrations

Random House 🏠 New York

Rubble wants

to be a super pup!

Rubble wants
to help someone.

Farmer Yumi needs help.

Her chickens are loose!

Rubble the Super Pup
will help!
He gets all the chickens
into their pen.

Rubble finds

Mayor Goodway next.

She needs help!

There was a rockslide.

A train is stuck

in the tunnel!

The mayor needs

the PAW Patrol to help.

Rubble runs
to the mountain.
"Where is the PAW Patrol?"
asks the engineer.

"Rubble the Super Pup
will save the day
his own way!"
says Rubble.

Rubble pushes the rocks.

More rocks fall!
Now both ends
of the tunnel
are blocked.

Rubble needs help.

He calls Ryder.

The PAW Patrol is
on the way!
Zuma drives
Rubble's digger.

Chase moves a rock.

Rubble is free!

Rubble uses his digger
to move the other
rocks.

The train is free!
The engineer thanks
Ryder and the pups.

Rubble is happy
the team helped him.
They saved the day
the PAW Patrol way!